The Thought Green Room

Written by K.A. Champagne (aka 'The Pie Man')
Image, design and edited by Pamela J. Salen

Construction Zone Ahead!

The Thought Green Room

The "Green Room" is a term used
for the waiting area for celebrities,
musicians or guests to relax before
they are called out onstage for their
appearance on a talk show or concert.

They usually sit around, some snacks
are available, they chit chat with the
other guests or fellow celebrities as
they wait for their turn to be called
on stage by the stage manager.

In this short story, I will refer to
the "Green Room" or "waiting area"
of the brain as a neighborhood.
We all have a "Green Room." It
exists in everyone's brain.

The "Thought Green Room" is a waiting area for words. It is the place where words wait to be called into use to help write sentences.

Sentences that can become paragraphs which allow you to speak, write letters, meet someone new, or to send a text message.

There are many words that already live in or wait in my Thought Green Room and more move in on a regular basis but only if I learn them and let them in.

Your neighborhood can be small or it can be large, depending on the size of your vocabulary.

Your vocabulary, the amount of words you have learned and sometimes use when speaking or writing, will determine the size of your word neighborhood.

Always remember, you are in charge. You are the boss and you are the stage manager.

In fact, you own this neighborhood. You control when and if a word will be called on stage to be spoken or written.

Here are a few of the words that live in my neighborhood. You may know some of them already, but as you know, neighborhoods are all different. They are all unique.

Unique

Unique sometimes doesn't even know it, but it is special. It doesn't always see itself in the mirror because most people who are truly unique don't even see it.

As you will learn there are all kinds of words that live in the Thought Green Room, in your neighborhood.

All of the words that you have
already read up to this point live
in my neighborhood, my Thought
Green Room. They were just sitting
around waiting for a job, waiting
to be called on stage by me.

I am the stage manager of my brain
because I decide what to say or write.

You are the stage manager of your
brain because you also decide what
to say or write. You tell words
when to get ready for the show.

I will explain as best I can a few
words that live in my neighborhood.
The others you will have to figure
out on your own. When you don't
understand the meaning of some
of these words, ask someone the
meaning. Better yet, use a dictionary.

The dictionary is kind of like the
security guard of my Thought Green
Room neighborhood. It has been a
great help to me in writing this story.

Although looking up a word takes time,
as you will also learn, most things
that are worthwhile aren't always
easy and usually do take time.

Time

Time is the most precious of all
commodities. It is even more precious
than gold. Sometimes it seems to
move like a turtle and appears on
occasion to move too slowly, but
like a turtle, time never stops until
it arrives at its final destination.

Some words hang out together
while waiting to be called on
stage or waiting to find work.

Some words sit side by side.

Some words are loners and
choose to sit alone.

Some words are happy.

Some words are sad.

Some words are angry.

Some words are always in
a good mood.

Each word is as important as
the other. For to find work in a
sentence, they must all get along,
whether they like it or not.

Hey, jobs are hard to come by and each
word waits anxiously to be called by
the stage manager of your brain.

Working together is way more
fun than sitting alone.

Here's an example of words, that
like it or not, hang out together.

Black and Blue

Black and Blue usually show up when
things aren't going well. Try to spot
these two guys as soon as possible.
For they can cause you much pain.

Give and Take

Give and Take should always be sent out at the same time. These two are necessary for all successful projects.

Pros and Cons

Additionally, we all know that discussing the Pros and Cons of any decision will usually lead to a better outcome.

I hope you can see how some words make it necessary for other words to follow quickly, and that without sending both together trouble can result.

Remember Black and Blue?

My neighborhood is very busy. In fact,
some days the traffic is so bad with
words coming and going that it's hard
for all of them to make it out of the
Thought Green Room and get to work.

Some of them are in such a hurry
that they sometimes leave too
quickly, half dressed, leaving
their true meaning behind.

When I am in a hurry or rush a
word out before thinking it through,
it usually gets me in trouble.

All words are powerful. So, take
your time when using them.

Words that leave too quickly can
be hurtful or misunderstood. They
usually get sent back home for re-
evaluation which cost time and money.

Sometimes they even lose their job.

Some words are used for the purpose of writing and some for speaking. Some of the speaking words are spoken softly and some are loud. My favorites are the ones that speak softly.

But first let me introduce you to the two loudest and most aggravating words that live in my neighborhood.

Rant and Rave

Rant and Rave are twins, although they do sometimes work alone, but rarely.

Occasionally, when someone goes on a mindless Rant, Rave stays home. That's when I see Rant get dressed and go to work.

Rant is usually very tired when he gets home and even though his job only lasts a short time, Rant always seems very exhausted.

When Rant works alone and Rave
stays at home she brags to everyone
that will listen about how her
brother has found some work.

Rave is always bragging and Rant,
sadly always seems angry.

Being angry must be a very exhausting
way of life because on his days off
Rant says nothing and usually sleeps
all night and late into the day.

Drunk and Stupid

Drunk and Stupid are cousins of
Rant and Rave. They sometimes
work along side each other.

Drunk and Stupid are also
twins and like their cousins
they sometimes work alone.

They almost always seem sad
and embarrassed after a night of
work. Although they sometimes
start out happy, they usually
end up very sad and sorry.

They usually work the night
shift, however I've seen them
called for work at all hours.

My suggestion is that you try your
hardest to avoid this family because
they will only bring you harm.

They are selfish and self-centered.

I know this because I have used them
on different jobs but I have found
that their work is sub par and I most
always have to employ new words to
repair the damage they have done.

Lazy

Lazy is also a relative of theirs, but I
don't often see him leave his house or
do much of anything except play games
on the computer or lay around on the
sofa changing channels on the TV.

The only thing I've heard him say is,
"I'm too tired" or "Where did I leave
that dang remote?" Too lazy to try
to find it, he usually falls asleep.

Smile and Happy

Smile and Happy are my two favorite
neighbors in my Thought Green Room.

A Smile can make me Happy and Happy
almost always makes me Smile.

They are very kind neighbors and
have on many occasions helped
me get through a tough day.

There are short words and long
words in the Thought Green Room.

Short words are not my favorites
because they are usually too simple
and boring although they are easier.
Easier is not always better.

So don't be afraid to use long words
because they can also get the
job done; kind of like an upgrade
from coach to first class.

Here are some examples of what I
mean by short words: he, she, it, go,
stop, stay, no, and of course, Yes.

Yes

Yes is one of my favorite words.
Because it means I've gotten my
way. And boy, do I like getting my
way. But it's not my true favorite.

Love

Love happens to be my most favorite
word and the best neighbor I've
ever had. We all need Love.

Love is very strong and powerful
and I have needed Love's
help on many occasions.

Hate

Hate is my least favorite word and the
worst neighbor I've ever had. Hate
can be very hurtful and usually is.

But even Hate has a good side, but
should only be used on rare occasions.

I'll give you an example,
"I just hate mean people."

This is not a great example because
Love almost always does a better job.

I've seen love turn hate into
a marshmallow. In fact, Love
can do most anything.

Admiration and Idolize

Love and Admiration sometimes
work together, but never confuse
Admiration with it cousin Idolize.

Idolize has poor eye sight and is
sometimes even totally blind.

To Admire someone for their talent
is okay, but to Idolize can on many
occasions cause you great harm.

Be very suspicious of these two
words because they can be very
tricky. They seem similar, but
I assure you they are not.

Now here are some examples of
"high-priced," "top shelf," "not
from around here" words.

Curmudgeon. Woebegone.
Discombobulate and of course one of
the most famous looooong words,
antidisestablishmentiarism.

These long words have become some
of my favorite neighbors of all.

Don't ever be afraid to let them
move into your Thought Green
Room, your neighborhood.

One reason is that they seem to be very
patient. Some of them have sat around
for years waiting to be called into duty.

But you see, all neighbors
deserve a job, including those
we don't understand at first.

I've had to learn to accept these words
slowly because to get to know these
neighbors can take a long time. Maybe
that's why they are called long words.

There are no borders or walls in my neighborhood. My Thought Green Room welcomes all words no matter the country of origin. Accents are enjoyed to the max because figuring them out is half the fun.

Habeas Corpus

I just love to say Habeas Corpus which is actually two medium size words that are most always used together.

Lawyers and Judges use them a lot, so they must work at a law firm.

I think I'll look them up in the dictionary later to see if I can find their true meaning.

Shhhh. Now what about the words with silent letters.

Like Gnome. Know. Knife. Phenomena. Whistle.

Shhhh.

Confidence

Confidence is a very proud word, but
one of the most important of them all.

Without Confidence almost
nothing gets done.

Short-changed

Short-changed, he may be hyphenated,
but beware, he'll steal you blind.

Hyphenated merely takes two smaller
words and joins them together to make
a long word with a deeper meaning.

Sometimes women do this when they
get married. They take their maiden
name, the last name they were born
with and hyphenate it with their new
husband's last name to create a new last
name, like Jones-Drew or Dunbar-Gates.

Now don't confuse these hyphenated
words with names like Mary Tyler
Moore or Martin Luther King.

Some people like to be known by
their full given names. They use
their middle name because it sets
them apart from Mary Moore and
Marty King, whoever they are?

Hippopotamus

The last long word that I will
give you is Hippopotamus.

I first met him at the zoo, but he
really comes from another country.

I don't see him too often and although
he owns a place in my neighborhood,
my Thought Green Room, he must have
rented an apartment at the zoo because
I rarely see him unless I visit a zoo or
watch a show on TV about animals.

I hope you introduce yourself to the
new neighbors that move into your
Thought Green Room and welcome
them with open arms. New neighbors
will be moving in every day.

It can be a rewarding experience.
However, always be careful to
remember that words are powerful.
To use them incorrectly can cause
great harm to you and to the rest of
the neighborhood, your neighborhood,
your Thought Green Room.

Some dirty words exist in my Thought
Green Room and have fought hard to get
into this story. I always try to exclude
them because they are too ignorant to
be given a seat in my Thought Green
Room, gosh darn it son of a gun.

I am grateful for my Thought
Green Room. It has taught
me great lessons and on most
occasions has served me well.

Your Thought Green Room can
do the same for you, but only if
you work hard at letting as many
new words as you can move in.

Wigwam

Wigwam, now that's a funny
sounding word. I wonder what it
means? I guess I'll have to ask my
security guard, the old dictionary
and welcome a new neighbor.

The End.

But not really because it's really
only the beginning, the beginning
of your Thought Green Room.

Construction zone ahead!

About the Author

K.A. Champagne is a poet, traveller, word-smith, comedian, survivor, middle-child, romantic, and kid-at-heart.

About the Designer

Pamela J. Salen is an artist, designer, educator, rock-collector, pattern-maker, seeker and hider, left-handed, and an identical twin.

Note: It was pointed out to me after the first printing of this short story that a word had been misspelled. I decided to leave it misspelled in the second printing. Can you find it?

comments welcome at:
weneedanap@ymail.com

49738167R00018